The Dragonsitter's Island

First published in 2014 by
Andersen Press Limited
20 Vauxhall Bridge Road
London SW1V 2SA
www.andersenpress.co.uk

2 4 6 8 10 9 7 5 3 1

British Library Cataloguing in Publication Data available.

ISBN 978 1 78344 045 0

Printed and bound in Great Britain by
CPI Group (UK) Ltd, Croydon, CR0 4YY

The Dragonsitter's Island

Josh Lacey

Illustrated by Garry Parsons

Andersen Press
London

Dear Uncle Morton

Where is the key to your house?

We arrived on your island this morning, but we couldn't get in.

Mum thought you might have left it under a stone or buried in a flowerpot, so we searched everywhere.

Emily discovered a silver necklace and I found one pound, but there was no sign of the key.

Through the window I could see your dragons going crazy. I don't know if they were happy to see us or just hungry, but Arthur was charging round and round the house, knocking over your furniture, and Ziggy wouldn't stop breathing fire.

1

Luckily Mr McDougall was still here. He was sure you wouldn't mind if he broke a window.

Unfortunately he couldn't open the front door from the inside, so we had to push the suitcases through the window and climb in after them.

Ziggy and Arthur are much happier now we've given them our presents (a big box of Maltesers for her and three packets of chocolate mini eggs for him).

They also ate our leftover sandwiches from the train and the book I was reading. Luckily it wasn't very good.

Emily and I are going to search your house for the key. Mum says if we can't find it, we'll have to go home tomorrow and the dragons can fend for themselves.

I said I wouldn't mind climbing in and out of the window for the whole week, but Mum told me not to be ridiculous.

Have you taken it by mistake? Didn't you leave a spare anywhere?

Love from

Your favourite nephew

Eddie

Dear Uncle Morton

We haven't found the key, but I have found your phone. Mum rang you to leave another message and I heard it ringing behind the sofa.

I hope you don't need it in Outer Mongolia. I put it on the mantelpiece with the necklace and the pound.

Mr McDougall has gone back to the mainland in his boat. Emily says it's creepy being the only people here, but I like it.

Thanks for your instructions and the map. Emily and Mum took hours unpacking their bags, so I've been exploring. I climbed Dead Man's Cairn and walked all the way along the beach to Lookout Point.

Arthur sat on my shoulder like a parrot. At first I was worried he might burn my ear off, but he hasn't been breathing any fire at all. Isn't he old enough?

Eddie

Dear Uncle Morton

We have now searched your house, your garden and quite a lot of your island, but we still can't find the key. Please write back ASAP and tell us where it is.

Mum is deadly serious about leaving tomorrow. It's not just because of the key. It's the poos too. Ziggy did one in the kitchen and another by the back door.

I know it's not her fault. She can't fit through the window and she has to go somewhere. I just wish she could hold them in till we've found the key.

Also Mum says where is the tin opener?

We brought some food, but not enough because you told us your cupboard was full of provisions. Unfortunately all the provisions are in tins.

I'm sure I could open them with a knife but Mum won't let me because we'd need a helicopter to get to the nearest hospital.

Eddie

Dear Uncle Morton

I'm very sorry, but we are leaving your island.

This morning Mum found another poo in the kitchen. She said that was the final straw.

I did suggest staying here on my own, but Mum said, "Not a chance, buster."

She has already raised the red flag. I just looked through the telescope and saw Mr McDougall preparing his boat on the mainland. I suppose he'll be here in about fifteen minutes.

I have given all our spare food to the dragons. I have also put some tins on the floor in case they're better at opening them than me.

I will ask Mr McDougall to come here every day and feed them till you get back.

Eddie

From: Edward Smith-Pickle

To: Morton Pickle

Date: Sunday 19 February

Subject: Sheep

Attachments: The prime suspects

Dear Uncle Morton

We're still here.

We never left. Mr McDougall wouldn't let us.

He said the dragons can't stay on your island unsupervised.

Mum asked why not, and Mr McDougall explained that one of his sheep went missing in the middle of the night. This morning he found bloodstains on the grass and a trail of wool leading down to the water.

I don't know why he blames your dragons. Arthur can hardly fly and Ziggy can't even leave the house, so there is no way either of them could have got from here to the mainland, let alone murdered a sheep. But Mr McDougall says they are the prime suspects.

Now he has gone home again and we're stuck here without a key or any food.

Eddie

From: Morton Pickle

To: Edward Smith–Pickle

Date: Monday 20 February

Subject: Re: Sheep

Attachments: The library; Airag and stew

Dear Eddie

I am so sorry to hear about your troubles with the front door. I was sure that I had discussed the key with your mother when we talked last week. Has she forgotten our conversation?

This is what I said to her. If you walk down to the end of the garden, you will discover a stone statue of a Yellow-headed Vulture perched in the heather. The key is hidden under its left talon.

Please be very careful when you lift it up. That vulture has great sentimental value. I was given it by the sculptor himself, who lives in a small hut beside the Amazon, and I carried it all the way back from Brazil wrapped in an old shirt.

I have been in touch with Mr McDougall, who is understandably upset about the loss of his sheep. I assured him that the dragons couldn't be responsible. He didn't appear to be entirely convinced, but I'm sure he'll find the real culprit soon.

All is good here in Ulaanbaatar. I have discovered some fascinating and unexpected information in the National Library, so my visit has already been worthwhile.

The only problem is the weather. Walking the streets without a coat would be certain death and even the Reading Room is so cold that no one removes their hats or scarves.

Unfortunately it's impossible to turn the pages of an old book while wearing gloves, so my fingers are like icicles by the end of the day. Every evening, after leaving the library, I warm myself up in a local restaurant with a bowl of yak stew and a glass of the local brew – a white drink called Airag, made from fermented horse milk. It tastes better than it sounds.

I'm very sorry about the tin opener. Have you looked in the cutlery drawer?

With love from

Your affectionate uncle

Morton

From: Edward Smith-Pickle

To: Morton Pickle

Date: Monday 20 February

Subject: Speedboat

Attachments: Mum and Emily

Dear Uncle Morton

We found the key!

And we were very careful with the statue.

Mum says you definitely didn't mention it last week. She would have remembered if you had.

You don't have to worry about the tin opener. It wasn't in the cutlery drawer or anywhere else, but Mr McDougall's nephew Gordon nipped across this morning in his speedboat and delivered another. He also brought a box of oatcakes and some nice cheese.

After he had gone, I found Mum and Emily whispering in the kitchen.

When I asked what was going on, Emily said they were talking about Gordon. Mum thinks he's very handsome.

I don't know if he's handsome, but I like his boat. He said he'll take me for a ride round the island to see the puffins.

Love from

Eddie

Dear Uncle Morton

Gordon has been here again. He took us to Lower Bisket in his speedboat to buy provisions.

Emily thinks it was a date.

Mum told her not to be ridiculous, but she did go bright pink.

Apparently Mr McDougall is on the rampage. Another sheep went missing last night.

I asked Gordon to tell him that the dragons spent the whole night in my bedroom with the door shut and the windows locked.

Gordon said I should do the same tonight because Mr McDougall is planning to stay up from dusk till dawn with a Thermos of hot tea and a rifle.

Otherwise everything is fine. We bought lots of food in the Lower Bisket General Store. The dragons are happy. Even Mum is in a good mood. We went for a walk on the beach this afternoon and she said it's so peaceful and beautiful she can almost understand why you want to live here.

Eddie

Dear Eddie

I have to admit that I was worried by your last message. I know from personal experience that Mr McDougall is an excellent shot.

On that particular occasion he wasn't aiming at me, but I should not like to find myself in his sights.

Please make sure that you keep the dragons under observation at all times. I cannot believe that they could be responsible for attacking his livestock but I wouldn't want to expose them to any unnecessary risks.

I hope your mother enjoyed her date with Gordon. Isn't he a little young for her?

Morton

Dear Uncle Morton

You don't have to worry about the dragons. I am keeping a close eye on them.

This morning I took them for a walk along the beach and I didn't let them out of my sight for a moment.

I told Mum what you said about Gordon being too young for her, and she said actually the age difference is only two years and ten months.

Today he took us to the Fish Museum in Arbothnot. He said it's the biggest attraction in the area.

I suppose it would be very interesting if you liked fish.

Afterwards Gordon bought us souvenirs in the museum shop. He got a plastic shark for me and a marine sticker book for Emily. He wanted to buy a pair of pearl earrings for Mum but she said they were too expensive, so he got her some smoked salmon instead.

He is coming back tomorrow for tea.

Emily asked if we would have to move to Scotland if they got married. Mum just laughed and said we will cross that bridge when we come to it.

Love from

Eddie

Dear Uncle Morton

The McDougalls are here.

Mum actually only invited Gordon but Mr McDougall came too.

He won't stop shouting and waving his arms.

He has lost three sheep in a week. Now he wants to take the dragons away and lock them in his barn till the police arrive.

I said he couldn't do that, but he said, "Don't you worry, laddie, it's perfectly legal."

I can't understand how it can be perfectly legal to steal someone else's dragons, but no one is taking any notice of me.

If you get this, please call us ASAP.

Someone has to stop Mr McDougall!

Eddie

From: Edward Smith–Pickle

To: Morton Pickle

Date: Thursday 23 February

Subject: Your shed

Attachments: The prisoners

Dear Uncle Morton

The McDougalls have gone.

Everyone argued for a long time and finally Mr McDougall agreed the dragons could stay here as long as they're locked up.

They are now in the shed.

Arthur is miserable. He keeps screaming and wailing and bashing his head against the door, trying to break it open.

I told him he's only in there for his own safety but he took no notice.

Mum says he'll calm down when he's had something to eat. We're going to open a few tins and give the dragons a special supper.

I hope Mr McDougall catches the sheep thief soon.

Eddie

Dear Uncle Morton

I'm very sorry, but your dragons have burned down your shed.

Emily and I were having breakfast when we smelled smoke. We ran outside and saw the whole thing blazing.

I put out the fire with buckets of water but there's not much left except a few black bits of wood.

There's no sign of your dragons either.

I'm afraid I can't build your shed again. I'm terrible at woodwork. Last time we did it at school, I put a nail through my knee.

But I will find your dragons, I promise.

Eddie

From: Edward Smith–Pickle

To: Morton Pickle

Date: Friday 24 February

Subject: Look!

📎 **Attachments:** The real sheep thief

Dear Uncle Morton

I have discovered who has been eating Mr McDougall's sheep!

It is the Loch Ness Monster.

I was actually looking for your dragons. I finally found them on the beach, mucking about on the sand as if nothing had happened. They didn't even look guilty.

I was just about to give them a proper telling-off when I happened to look out to sea, and I saw this!

I shall tell Mr McDougall as soon as I see him.

Eddie

Dear Eddie

Thank you for the photo. I'm not an expert, but I would say it's a swan.

Don't worry about Mr McDougall's sheep or who might be eating them. Keeping the dragons safe is much more important. Could you lock them in the house?

Of course you'll have to let them out every now and then to stretch their wings and go to the loo, but please make sure they don't run away again.

The livestock laws are very clear. If Mr McDougall caught them anywhere near his sheep, he would have a perfect right to shoot them.

My work here is almost done. Last night

I was lucky enough to have dinner with Professor Ganbaataryn Baast, and he has invited me to accompany him on an expedition to the Altai mountains this summer, searching for a famous family of dragons. Apparently they live in an enormous cave stuffed with gold. No man has ever seen it and lived to tell the tale. Professor Baast intends to be the first – and I shall be the second!

Morton

Dear Uncle Morton

It is not a swan. It's definitely the Loch Ness Monster. I've got a book about Famous Mysteries at home and I recognise it from the pictures.

I'm going to search your island for it.

If I get a better photo, I can prove to Mr McDougall who has really been stealing his sheep, and he'll stop blaming Ziggy and Arthur.

I asked Mum and Emily to help but they're not interested. They don't even believe I've seen the Loch Ness Monster.

In fact Mum thinks I'm making up stories because of Gordon.

After lunch she sat me down for a serious talk. She said Gordon isn't her boyfriend but she might get a boyfriend one day and would I mind?

I said Dad has a new girlfriend every time we see him, so who cares?

Anyway, even if I was upset about Mum having a boyfriend, why would I make up stories about the Loch Ness Monster?

Eddie

Dear Uncle Morton

I borrowed your boat. I hope you don't mind. I was very careful.

I took the dragons too. I know you want
them to stay locked up, but they'll actually
be safer with me. I won't let them out of
my sight.

We rowed into the middle of the sea, but
there was no sign of the monster.

I would have rowed the whole way round
the island, but I didn't want to get swept
out to sea. So I rowed back to your jetty
and tied up the boat, then started walking.

I found:

A bird's nest with three eggs.

A whole tree washed up on the beach.

A wrecked boat buried in the sand.

A starfish (dead).

Six crabs (still alive).

Some puffins.

And about a thousand seagulls.

Unfortunately there was no sign of Nessie.

Do you know any caves where she might be hiding?

Eddie

From: Morton Pickle
To: Edward Smith–Pickle
Date: Friday 24 February
Subject: Re: Nessie

Dear Eddie

Please don't be offended if I say this, but I really don't think you have seen the Loch Ness Monster.

A few years ago, I made a study of the myths and legends surrounding that fabulous beast. I wondered whether it might be a dragon, or a distant relative of the dragon which had somehow become aquatic.

Sadly I discovered that there is no reliable evidence that the monster has ever existed. All the sightings are, I'm afraid to say, the work of drunks, maniacs, frauds, fantasists and publicity-seekers of one sort or another.

I wish the monster did exist, but it doesn't. And even if it did, it would be swimming around Loch Ness, not my island.

In the years that I've been living there, I have spotted whales, dolphins, seals and even the occasional otter, so you may have been lucky enough to see one of them.

I don't know who or what has been stealing Mr McDougall's sheep but I can tell you one thing for certain: it is not Nessie.

Morton

From: Edward Smith–Pickle

To: Morton Pickle

Date: Friday 24 February

Subject: Re: Re: Nessie

Attachments: Evidence

If the monster doesn't exist, what's this?

Eddie

I'm coming home! Will change my tickets and catch next plane!

Do not approach the monster till I get there! It might be dangerous!

M

From: Edward Smith-Pickle

To: Morton Pickle

Date: Saturday 25 February

Subject: On the beach

Attachments: Flying practice; Air raid

Dear Uncle Morton

You're right about the monster. It is dangerous. In fact it's bloodthirsty.

It just tried to eat Arthur.

Ziggy was curled up on the sofa with Emily and Mum, watching some old movie. Arthur and I didn't want to see it so we went down on the beach again. I was using your binoculars to search for the Loch Ness Monster and Arthur was practising his flying.

He kept running along the sand and jumping into the air, then flapping his wings to stay up for as long as possible.

I tried to persuade him to land on the beach because rescuing him from the water is no fun at all, but he didn't take much notice.

One time he veered in the wrong direction and headed straight out to sea. I called at him to come back but he just flew further and further from the shore, as if he was trying to get all the way to the mainland.

Suddenly there was a great burst of water and the monster rose out of the waves, its long neck stretching into the air and its huge mouth opening to reveal two rows of glistening white teeth.

Snap!

It tried to take a bite out of Arthur. Just in time he dodged out of the way.

Snap! Snap!

The monster went for him again and again. Each time Arthur twisted through the air like a fighter pilot. I'd never seen him move so fast.

Finally he managed to point himself in the right direction and head back to the shore.

The monster charged after him. Both of them were coming straight for me.

Once they reached dry land, the monster couldn't move so quickly. It just waddled up the shore, flapping its flippers on the sand.

Arthur crashlanded at my feet. I could see he was absolutely exhausted by the effort of so much flying. I picked him up and tucked him under my arm and we ran all the way home.

From now on I'm going to follow your advice. I won't go anywhere near the monster till you get back.

Eddie

From: Morton Pickle

To: Edward Smith–Pickle

Date: Saturday 25 February

Subject: Re: On the beach

Dear Eddie

I am writing this from Ulaanbaatar airport. The runways are covered in thick snow and slippery ice, so my flight has been delayed. Apparently we should be boarding within the next hour.

I have to change planes in Moscow and Copenhagen, but if all goes well I shall be back in Edinburgh tomorrow morning and home in time for lunch.

I'm glad to hear you're going to keep away from the monster. Perhaps you should stay inside the house till I get back.

Morton

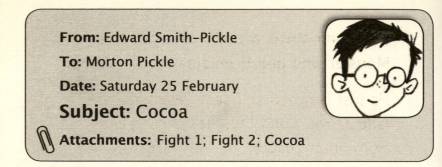

Dear Uncle Morton

You don't have to come home early if you don't want to.

Everything is fine here now. The monster has gone and Mr McDougall has forgiven your dragons.

He wasn't so friendly earlier. He arrived in his rowing boat with Gordon, ready to arrest Ziggy and Arthur.

He had been watching us through his binoculars and saw them snoozing on the grass. He said if we couldn't keep them safely locked up, he would take them straight to the police station in Upper Bucket.

I told him it was actually the Loch Ness Monster who had been stealing his sheep.

He just laughed and said, "Are you sure, laddie? You don't think it's those aliens from outer space?"

I said he should come and see the monster for himself, and he said maybe he would after he'd arrested the dragons.

He tied a rope round Arthur's neck and marched him down to the boat. Ziggy kept snapping at his legs and blowing little spurts of flame in his direction, but she didn't bite his head off or set him on fire. I suppose she was worried about hurting Arthur too.

Gordon tried to stop his uncle, and so did Mum, but Mr McDougall wouldn't listen. He said he couldn't afford to lose another sheep and did they want to bankrupt him?

When we got to the jetty, Mr McDougall put Arthur in the bottom of the boat and

Ziggy jumped in after them. I tried to climb in too, but Gordon grabbed me round the middle and said, "Not so fast."

Mr McDougall dipped his oars and rowed out to sea. We were all shouting at him – me and Emily and Mum and Gordon – but he took no notice. He just headed for the mainland.

The waves got bigger. The boat was rolling around. I was really worried it might tip over and Arthur would drown.

They were almost halfway between the island and the mainland when the monster attacked. It seemed to come from nowhere. It lifted its head out of the water, opened its mouth and lunged at them.

Mr McDougall tried to defend himself with one of the oars but the monster bit the end off. Then it took a big chunk out of the boat.

It would have eaten them all if Ziggy hadn't fought back. She was amazing!

She flapped her wings and lifted into the air, then breathed a great big ball of fire straight at the monster's head.

I've never seen anyone look so surprised.

The monster floated there for a moment, its scales smouldering. Then it raised itself out of the waves and struck again.

The battle was terrible. But I always knew who would win. And I was right.

Every time the monster tried to bite Ziggy, she flew out of its way, then turned round and blew back another blazing fireball. Soon the Loch Ness Monster was black and burnt and smoking from the top of its head to the tip of its tail.

Finally it plunged under the waves and disappeared in a cloud of bubbles.

Ziggy dragged Arthur and Mr McDougall back to shore. She couldn't swim very fast with them holding her wings but that didn't matter. At least they were safe.

Mr McDougall wasn't very happy about leaving his boat behind, but it was already smashed to pieces and just about to sink.

When they finally got to the beach, Mr McDougall lay on the sand for a minute or two, getting his breath back. Then he rolled over and said, "I owe you an apology, laddie."

I told him my name is actually Eddie and he promised to call me that from now on.

He said sorry to the dragons too.

Now we're all inside your house. I hope you don't mind, but Mr McDougall has borrowed some of your dry clothes.

Mum is making cocoa for everyone, the dragons included.

Eddie

Hi E

I'm changing planes in Moscow.

Just checked timetables and should be home on 15.37 train – could you ask Gordon to meet me?

Glad to hear you're all safe. Please be very careful till I get there. The monster might come back.

M

Dear Uncle Morton

You don't have to worry about the monster. I'm sure it won't be coming back.

Even if it does, Ziggy will chase it away again.

Gordon came to meet your train at 15.37 but there was no sign of you. Did you miss your plane?

We have been packing up and getting ready to leave tomorrow.

I'd like to stay on your island for another week but school starts on Tuesday, so Mum says we have to go home.

Eddie

Dear Uncle Morton

Gordon got your message about the plane and the train. He will be waiting for you tomorrow at 9.01.

Our train leaves at 9.27, so we'll just have time to say hello and goodbye.

We're all packed and ready to go. I'm very sad to be leaving your island but our last night has been brilliant. We had a barbecue on the beach – Mr McDougall, the dragons, Emily and me.

Mum wasn't there. She went to a restaurant on the mainland with Gordon.

This time it really was a date. Mum was very worried because she hadn't brought

any smart clothes, but Emily and I told
her it didn't matter because she looked
beautiful how she was.

And she did. When she was standing on the
jetty, waiting for Gordon to pick her up in
his speedboat, she looked like someone in
a movie.

Once they'd gone, Emily and I collected driftwood on the beach, Ziggy lit the fire and Mr McDougall cooked the best barbie ever.

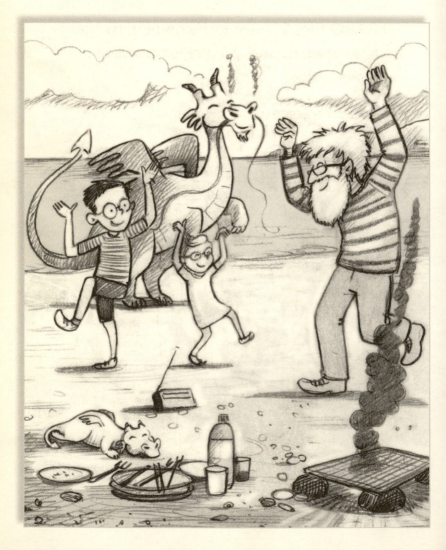

Mr McDougall has entirely forgiven your dragons. He says Ziggy is a bonnie lass and she's welcome to as many lamb cutlets as she wants.

The McDougalls have gone home now but they're coming back to pick us up in the morning.

See you tomorrow!

Eddie

From: Morton Pickle

To: Edward Smith-Pickle

Date: Tuesday 28 February

Subject: Re: Our last night

Attachments: Two happy dragons

Dear Eddie

I was so sorry to miss you yesterday.
My plane was delayed again and I finally
got to the station at three o'clock in the
afternoon. Luckily Gordon was still waiting
for me.

Ziggy and Arthur are both in fine spirits.

They've obviously had a very happy week.
Thank you for looking after them so well.

I brought some presents from Outer
Mongolia to say thank you. I shall send
them by first class post.

The McDougalls and I patrolled the
shore last night, armed with torches and
shotguns, but the monster did not return.
I do hope she'll come back soon. I would
love to see her for myself.

As you know, Gordon was eager to contact
the newspapers but I persuaded him not
to. For one thing, I don't want hordes of
reporters swarming across my island.
For another, despite her ferocity, Nessie
deserves some privacy.

Apparently Mr McDougall did tell the whole
pub about her but everyone just thought
he'd had too many whiskies.

We have now agreed she will remain our
secret. I suggest you do the same.

I have not quizzed Gordon on other matters but I gather he has been in touch with your mother, and may be visiting you at some point. Perhaps he could bring the dragons? Or would you like to come and stay again? All of us would be delighted to see you.

Morton

From: Edward Smith-Pickle

To: Morton Pickle

Date: Thursday 2 March

Subject: Home

📎 **Attachments:** Scarf; Slippers

Dear Uncle Morton

We're back home too. Our house and our garden feel very small compared to your island, but it's nice to see my stuff again.

I think you're right about keeping quiet about the monster. My book about Famous Mysteries says Loch Ness is packed with scientists and tourists. You wouldn't want them on your island. In fact, that's probably why she decided to leave Loch Ness in the first place.

I had already shown the photos to Miss Brackenbury, but I've asked her not to tell anyone. She said our secret is safe with her.

65

Thank you very much for the presents from Outer Mongolia. Emily has been wearing her cashmere scarf non-stop, and I really like my slipper. Please do send the other one if you discover where Arthur hid it.

Mum hasn't tried the Airag yet. She's keeping it for a special occasion.

I talked to Mum about coming back to your island and she says we'll see. That usually means no, but I think this time it might mean yes.

Love from

Eddie

From: Morton Pickle

To: Edward Smith–Pickle

Date: Wednesday 24 May

Subject: Fwd: One of yours?

Attachments: Clipping

Hi Eddie

I was sent this by a friend in Australia and thought you might be interested!

M

ADELAIDE DAILY NEWS

Tuesday 23rd May

Dinosaur spotted on popular Adelaide beach

Swimmers and holidaymakers were shocked yesterday by the sudden appearance of a mysterious beast on Semaphore Beach.

More than a hundred people fled from the water when an unidentified creature was spotted swimming about twenty metres from the shore.

Reports say that the beast had a small head, a long neck, an enormous brown body and little flippers. Some witnesses described it as looking like a dinosaur, leading experts to wonder if a previously unknown species could have been living on the shores of Australia for the past sixty million years. Beachgoers have been warned to stay out of the water all along Adelaide's beachfront until scientists and experts have studied photographs and footage of the unknown intruder. No one was hurt and the creature only stayed for a few minutes, leading to speculation that it might have been a trick of the light, a strangely-shaped piece of driftwood or even a great white shark covered in seaweed.

Local resident Gav McPherson remains baffled. "We're used to sharks and sea lions here. Killer jellyfish are no problem either. But this was something else, mate. I've never seen anything like it."

Police Chief Tina O'Sullivan says her department is keeping an open mind until further investigations have been completed. She refused to comment on speculation that the sighting could be linked to a series of sheep thefts in the area.

The Dragonsitter's Castle

Josh Lacey

Illustrated by Garry Parsons

'Dear Uncle Morton, your dragons are still here. They have eaten the entire contents of the fridge and most of the tins in the cupboard too.

Arthur also swallowed three spoons and the remote control. Mum says they will probably come out the other end, but I'm not really looking forward to that.'

Dragonsitting isn't getting any easier for Eddie. A castle, a sneezing dragon and a big box of fireworks. Looks like the new year is going to start with a bang!

Praise for *The Dragonsitter*:
'Short, sharp and funny'
Telegraph

9781849397698 £4.99